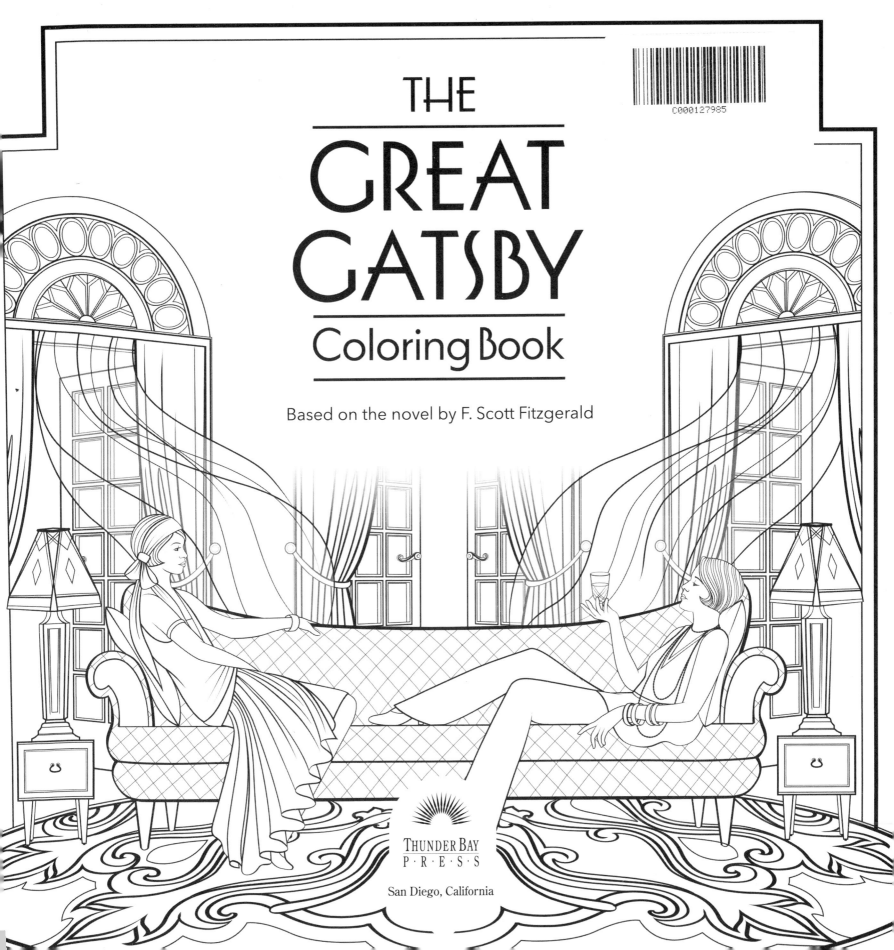

THE
GREAT
GATSBY
Coloring Book

Based on the novel by F. Scott Fitzgerald

THUNDER BAY
P·R·E·S·S

San Diego, California

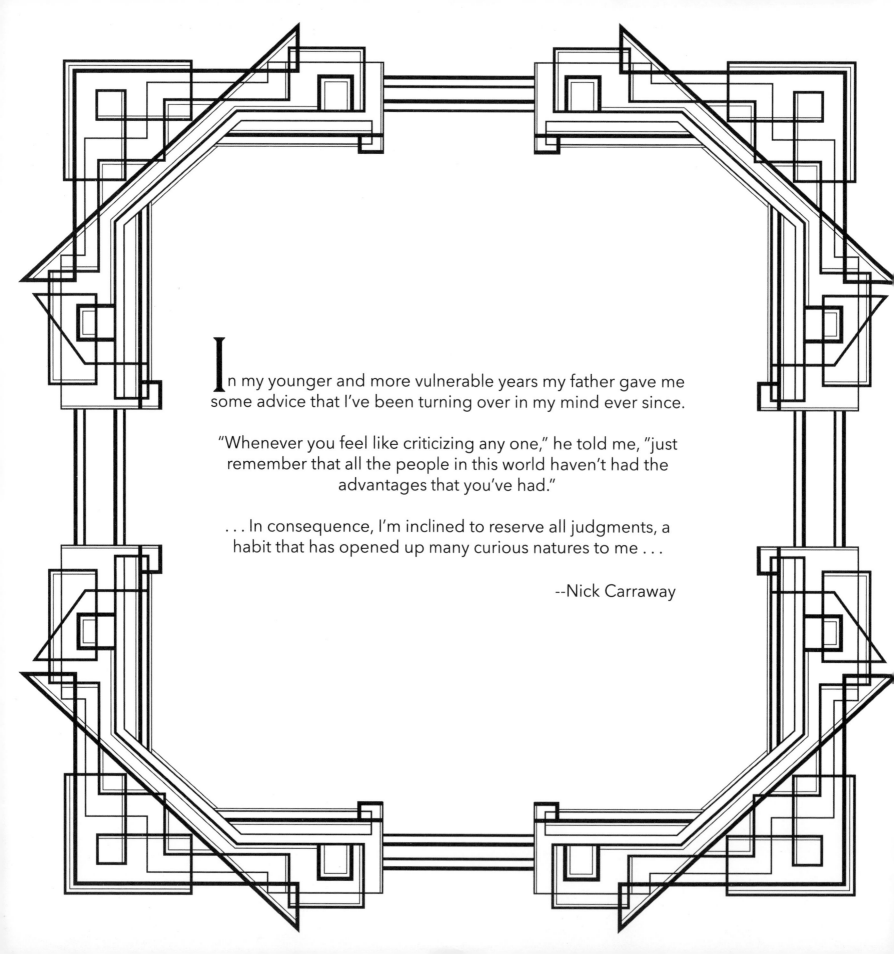

In my younger and more vulnerable years my father gave me some advice that I've been turning over in my mind ever since.

"Whenever you feel like criticizing any one," he told me, "just remember that all the people in this world haven't had the advantages that you've had."

. . . In consequence, I'm inclined to reserve all judgments, a habit that has opened up many curious natures to me . . .

--Nick Carraway

I lived at West Egg, only fifty yards from the Sound, and squeezed between two huge places that rented for twelve or fifteen thousand a season. The one on my right was a colossal affair by any standard—it was a factual imitation of some Hôtel de Ville in Normandy, with a tower on oneside, spanking new under a thin beard of raw ivy, and marble swimming pool, and more than forty acres of lawn and garden. It was Gatsby's mansion.

Across the courtesy bay the white palaces of fashionable East Egg glittered along the water, and the history of the summer really begins on the evening I drove over there to have dinner with the Tom Buchanans.

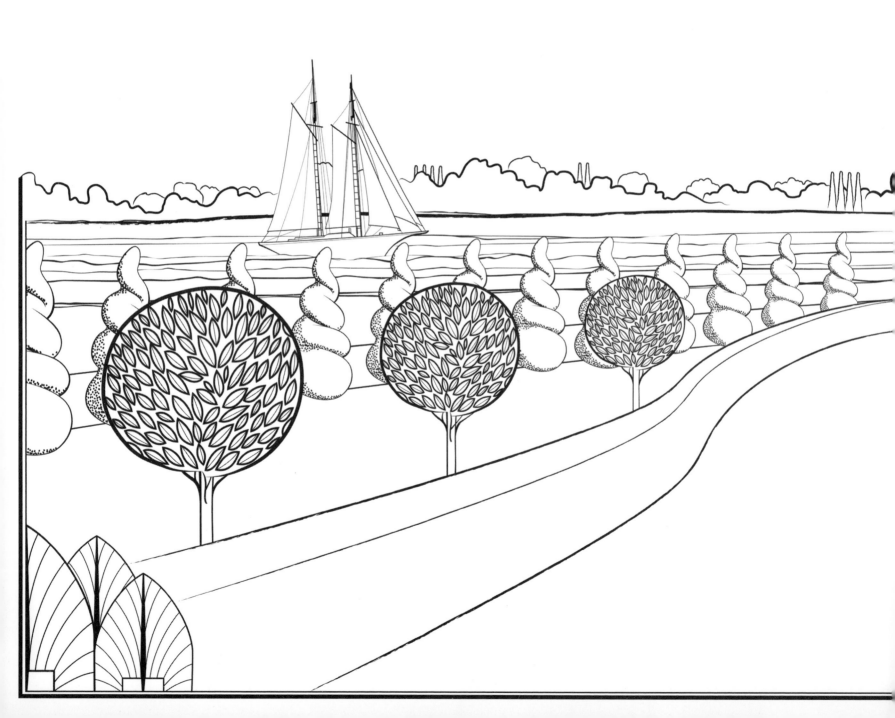

Daisy was my second cousin once removed, and I'd known Tom in college—one of the most powerful ends that ever played football at New Haven. His family were enormously wealthy, but now he'd left Chicago and come East in a fashion that rather took your breath away; for instance, he'd brought a string of polo ponies from Lake Forest.

We walked through a high hallway into a bright rosy-colored space. A breeze blew through the room. The only completely stationary object was an enormous couch on which two young women were buoyed up as though upon an anchored balloon.

Daisy made an attempt to rise, then she laughed, an absurd, charming little laugh . . . "I'm p-paralyzed with happiness." She laughed again, as if she said something very witty. She hinted in a murmur that the surname of the balancing girl was Baker.

I looked at Miss Baker . . . "You live in West Egg," she remarked contemptuously. "I know somebody there. You must know Gatsby."

"Gatsby?" demanded Daisy. "What Gatsby?"

Before I could reply that he was my neighbor dinner was announced. Tom compelled me from the room. The two young women preceded us out onto a rosy-colored porch open toward the sunset, where four candles flickered on the table in the diminished wind.

The telephone rang inside. The butler came and murmured something close to Tom's ear, whereupon Tom frowned, pushed back his chair, and without a word went inside. . . . Then suddenly Daisy threw her napkin on the table and excused herself and went into the house.

Miss Baker and I exchanged a short glance. She sat up alertly and said, "Sh! . . . Don't talk. I want to hear what happens . . . Tom's got some woman in New York." Almost before I had grasped her meaning there was the flutter of a dress and the crunch of leather boots, and Tom and Daisy were back at the table.

I followed Daisy around a chain of connecting verandas to the porch in front. In its deep gloom we sat down side by side on a wicker settee. I asked what I thought would be some sedative questions about her little girl.

"She was less than an hour old and Tom was God knows where. I woke up out of the ether with an utterly abandoned feeling, and asked the nurse right away . . . She told me it was a girl, and so I turned my head away and wept. 'All right,' I said, 'I'm glad it's a girl. And I hope she'll be a fool—that's the best thing a girl can be in this world, a beautiful little fool.'" The instant her voice broke off, I felt the basic insincerity of what she had said. I waited, and sure enough, in a moment she looked at me with an absolute smirk on her lovely face.

Inside, the crimson room bloomed with light. Tom and Miss Baker sat at either end of the long couch.

"Ten o'clock," Miss Baker remarked. "Time for this good girl to go to bed."

"Jordan's going to play in the tournament tomorrow," explained Daisy, "over at Westchester."

"Oh—you're Jordan Baker," I said. I knew now why her face was familiar—its expression had looked out at me from many rotogravure pictures of the sporting life at Asheville and Hot Springs and Palm Beach.

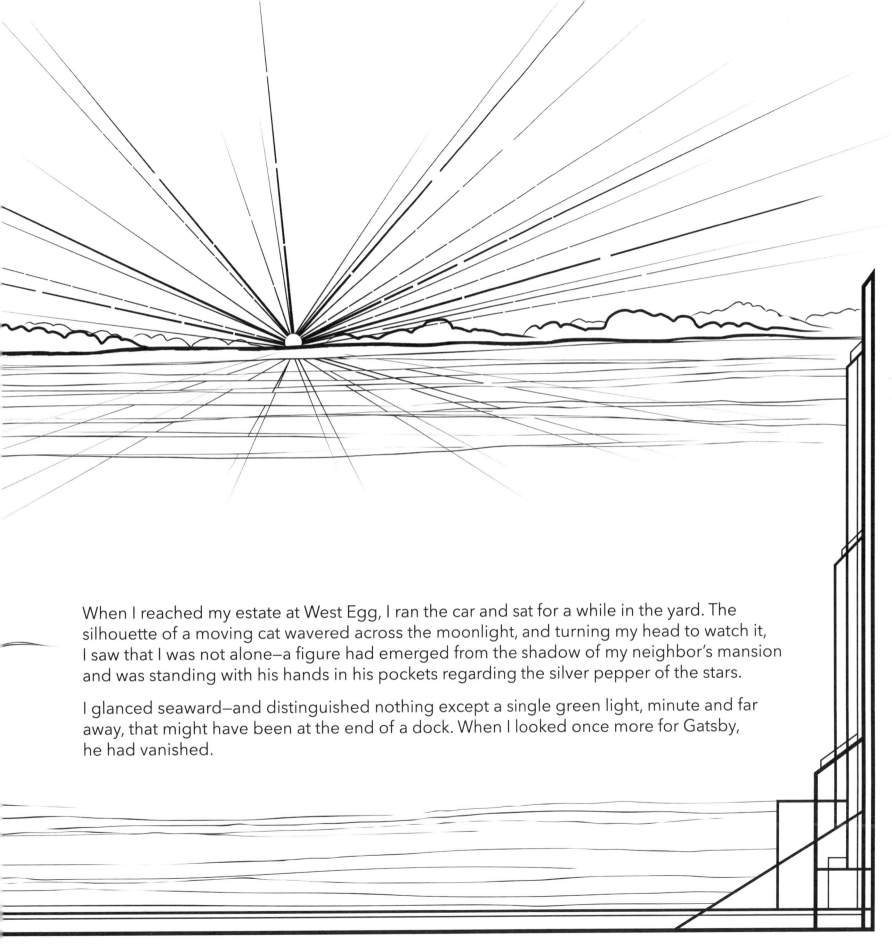

When I reached my estate at West Egg, I ran the car and sat for a while in the yard. The silhouette of a moving cat wavered across the moonlight, and turning my head to watch it, I saw that I was not alone—a figure had emerged from the shadow of my neighbor's mansion and was standing with his hands in his pockets regarding the silver pepper of the stars.

I glanced seaward—and distinguished nothing except a single green light, minute and far away, that might have been at the end of a dock. When I looked once more for Gatsby, he had vanished.

About halfway between West Egg and New York the motor road hastily joins the railroad and runs beside it. Above the gray land you perceive the eyes of Doctor T. J. Eckleburg—blue and gigantic looking out from a pair of enormous yellow spectacles which pass over a non-existent nose.

I went up to New York with Tom on the train one afternoon, and when we stopped he jumped to his feet and, taking hold of my elbow, literally forced me from the train. "We're getting off," he insisted. "I want you to meet my girl."

I followed Tom inside the garage. When Mr. Wilson went to get chairs, Mrs. Wilson moved close to Tom. Tom whispered, "I want to see you. Get on the next train. I'll meet you by the news-stand on the lower level."
So Tom Buchanan and his girl and I went up together to New York—or not quite together, for Mrs. Wilson sat discreetly in another car.

At 158th Street the cab stopped at one slice in a long white cake of apartment-houses. Throwing a regal homecoming glance, Mrs. Wilson went haughtily in.

The apartment was on the top floor. The living room was crowded to the doors with a set of tapestried furniture entirely too large for it. Mrs. Wilson had changed her costume and was now attired in an elaborate afternoon dress. Soon we were joined by her sister, Catherine, and the McKees, upstairs neighbors Mrs. Wilson had hastily invited.

I have been drunk just twice in my life, and the second time was that afternoon, that turned into evening, until I found myself half-asleep in the cold lower level of the Pennsylvania Station, waiting for the four o'clock train.

There was music from my neighbor's house through the summer nights.
In his blue gardens men and girls came and went like moths among
the whisperings and the champagne and the stars.

On buffet tables, garnished with glistening hors-d'oeuvre, spiced baked hams crowded against salads of harlequin designs and pastry pigs and turkeys bewitched to a dark gold.

The orchestra was no thin five-piece affair, but a whole pitful of oboes and trombones and saxophones and viols and cornets and piccolos, and low and high drums.

Dear Mr. Carraway,
The honour would be mine if
you would attend my party
yours sincerely
J Gatsby

I believe that on the first night I went to Gatsby's house,
I was one of the few guests who had actually been invited.
A chauffeur in a uniform of robin's-egg blue crossed my
lawn early that Saturday morning with a formal note
from his employer.

Dressed up in white flannels I went over to his lawn a little after seven, and wandered around rather ill at ease among swirls and eddies of people I didn't know, when Jordan Baker came out of the house. Welcome or not, I found it necessary to attach myself to someone.

By midnight the hilarity had increased. A celebrated tenor had sung in Italian and a notorious contralto had sung in jazz, and between the numbers people were doing "stunts" all over the garden, while happy, vacuous bursts of laughter rose toward the summer sky.

I was still with Jordan Baker. We were sitting at a table with a man about my age. "Your face is familiar," he said, politely. "Weren't you in the Third Division during the war?" When I confirmed I was, he said, "I knew I'd seen you somewhere before . . . I'm Gatsby." Almost at that moment, a butler hurried toward him with a message, and he excused himself with a small bow.

Later, my eyes fell on Gatsby again, standing alone on the marble steps and looking from one group to another when Gatsby's butler was suddenly standing beside us. "Miss Baker?" he inquired. "I beg your pardon, but Mr. Gatsby would like to speak to you alone."

As I waited for my hat in the hall the door of the library opened, and Jordan Baker and Gatsby came out together. She lingered for a moment to shake my hand.
"I've just heard the most amazing thing," she whispered. "Please come and see me . . ."
She was hurrying off as she talked.

Reading over what I have written so far, I see I have given the impression that the events of three nights several weeks apart were all that absorbed me. On the contrary, they were merely casual events in a crowded summer, and, until much later, they absorbed me infinitely less than my personal affairs.

Most of the time I worked at Probity Trust, where I knew the other clerks and young bondsalesmen by their first names and lunched with them. I took dinner usually at the Yale Club, and then went upstairs to the library and studied investments and securities.

At nine o'clock, one morning late in July, Gatsby's gorgeous cream-colored car lurched up the rocky drive to my door. It was the first time he had called on me, though I had gone to two of his parties and made use of his beach. "Good morning, old sport," he said. "You're having lunch with me today, and I thought we'd ride up together."

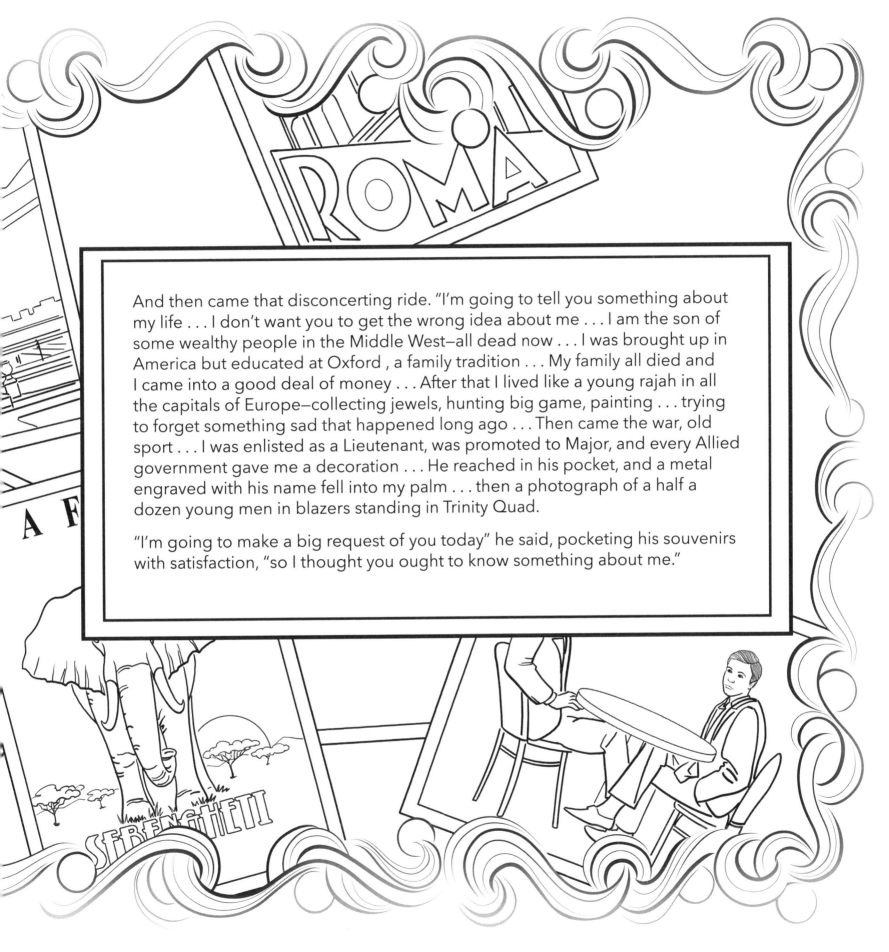

And then came that disconcerting ride. "I'm going to tell you something about my life . . . I don't want you to get the wrong idea about me . . . I am the son of some wealthy people in the Middle West–all dead now . . . I was brought up in America but educated at Oxford , a family tradition . . . My family all died and I came into a good deal of money . . . After that I lived like a young rajah in all the capitals of Europe–collecting jewels, hunting big game, painting . . . trying to forget something sad that happened long ago . . . Then came the war, old sport . . . I was enlisted as a Lieutenant, was promoted to Major, and every Allied government gave me a decoration . . . He reached in his pocket, and a metal engraved with his name fell into my palm . . . then a photograph of a half a dozen young men in blazers standing in Trinity Quad.

"I'm going to make a big request of you today" he said, pocketing his souvenirs with satisfaction, "so I thought you ought to know something about me."

"I happened to find out that you're taking Miss Baker to tea this afternoon, and she has kindly consented to speak to you about this matter." I was more annoyed than interested. I hadn't invited Jordan to tea in order to discuss Gatsby.

After our lunch I insisted on paying the check. As the waiter brought my change, I caught sight of Tom Buchanan across the crowded room.

When he saw us, Tom jumped up and took half a dozen steps in our direction. "Where've you been?" Tom demanded. "Daisy's furious because you haven't called up." I turned toward Mr. Gatsby, but he was no longer there.

One October day in nineteen-seventeen—(said Jordan Baker, sitting up very straight on a straight chair in the tea-garden at the Plaza Hotel)—I was walking from one place to another, half on the sidewalks and half on the lawns . . .

The largest of the lawns belonged to Daisy Fay's house. She was just eighteen, and by far the most popular of all the young girls in Louisville. She had a little white roadster, and all day long the telephone rang in her house and excited young officers from Camp Taylor demanded the privilege of monopolizing her that night.

When I came to her house that morning, her white roadster was beside the curb, and she was sitting in it with a lieutenant I had never seen before. His name was Jay Gatsby, and I didn't lay eyes on him again for over four years.

By the next year, wild rumors were circulating about Daisy—how her mother had found her packing her bag to go to New York to say good-by to a soldier who was going overseas. She was prevented, and after that she didn't play around with the soldiers any more.

By the next autumn, she was gay again. She had a début after the Armistice, and in February, she was presumably engaged to a man from New Orleans.

In June she married Tom Buchanan of Chicago, with more pomp and circumstance than Louisville ever knew before.

I was a bridesmaid. I came into her room half an hour before the bridal dinner, and found her as drunk as a monkey. She had a bottle of Sauterne in one hand and a letter in the other.

"Tell 'em all Daisy's change' her mine!" She began to cry—and she cried and cried.

I found her mother's maid, and we got her into a cold bath. She wouldn't let go of the letter.

She took it into the tub with her and squeezed it up into a wet ball. We gave her spirits of ammonia and put ice on her forehead . . . The next day at five o'clock, she married Tom Buchanan.

I saw them when they came back from a three-month honeymoon in the South Seas. I thought I'd never seen a girl so mad about her husband. It was touching to see them together. That was in August. A week later, Tom ran into a wagon on the Ventura road one night. The girl who was with him got into the papers too because her arm was broken—she was one of the chambermaids in the Santa Barbara Hotel.

The next April, Daisy had her little girl, and they went to France for a year. Then they came back to Chicago to settle down. Daisy was popular in Chicago. They moved with a fast crowd, all of them young and rich and wild, but she came out of it with a perfect reputation.

About six weeks ago, she heard the name Gatsby for the first time in years. It was when I asked you if you knew Gatsby in West Egg. After you went home she came into my room and said "What Gatsby?" It wasn't until then that I connected this Gatsby with the officer in her white car.

"It was a strange coincidence," I said.

"But it wasn't a coincidence at all. Gatsby bought that house so that Daisy would be just across the bay."

"Gatsby wants to know," continued Jordan, "if you'll invite Daisy to your house some afternoon and then let him come over."

The modesty of the demand shook me. "Why didn't he ask you to arrange a meeting?"

"He wants her to see his house," she explained, "And your house is right next door. He half expected her to wander into one of his parties, but she never did. Then he began asking people if they knew her, and I was the first one he found. She's not to know about it. You're just supposed to invite her to tea."

I called up Daisy the next morning and invited her to come to tea. "Don't bring Tom," I warned her.

The day we agreed upon was pouring rain. At eleven o'clock a man in a raincoat dragging a lawn-mower tapped at my door. At two o'clock a greenhouse arrived from Gatsby's, with innumerable receptacles to contain it. An hour later, Gatsby, in a white flannel suit, silver shirt, and gold-colored tie, hurried in.

At four o'clock, there was the sound of a motor turning into my lane. Gatsby and I jumped up, and I went out into the yard to meet Daisy. As we entered, to my overwhelming surprise, the living-room was deserted.

Soon there was a light dignified knocking at the front door. Gatsby, pale as death, was standing in a puddle of water. He stalked by me into the hall and disappeared into the living-room.

For half a minute there wasn't a sound, then I heard a sort of choking murmur, followed by Daisy's voice, "I certainly am awfully glad to see you again."

Amid the welcome confusion of cups and cakes a certain physical decency established itself. I made an excuse at the first possible moment and got to my feet. I walked out the back way— and ran for a huge black knotted tree. After a half hour, the sun shone again, and I went in. Daisy's face was smeared with tears.

"I want you and Daisy to come over to my house, old sport" Gatsby said. "I'd like to show her around."

It was strange to reach the marble steps and find no stir of bright dresses in and out the door, and hear no sound but bird voices in the trees.

And inside . . . he hadn't once ceased looking at Daisy, and I think he revalued everything in his house according to the measure of response it drew from her well-loved eyes.

His bedroom was the simplest room of all—except where the dresser was garnished with a toilet set of pure dull gold. He opened two hulking patent cabinets which held his massed suits and dressing-gowns and ties, and his shirts, piled like bricks in stacks a dozen high.

He took out a pile of shirts and began throwing them, one by one . . .

"They're such beautiful shirts," Daisy sobbed, her voice muffled in the thick folds. "It makes me sad because I've never seen such—such beautiful shirts before."

About this time an ambitious young reporter from New York arrived one morning at Gatsby's door and asked him if he had anything to say. Gatsby's notoriety, spread about by the hundreds who had accepted his hospitality and so become authorities on his past, had increased all summer until he fell short of being news.

James Gatz--was really, or at least legally, his name. His parents were shiftless and unsuccessful farm people—his imagination had never really accepted them as his parents at all. He told me all this much later, but I've put it down here, to clear this set of misconceptions about him.

For several weeks I didn't see Gatsby, but finally I went over to his house one Sunday afternoon. I was startled when someone brought Tom Buchanan in for a drink. The really surprising thing was that it hadn't happened before.

"I know your wife," Gatsby stated, almost aggressively . . . and after two drinks, it was agreed that Tom and his companions would all come over to Gatsby's next party.

Tom and Daisy arrived at twilight, and together, we strolled out among the sparkling hundreds.

Daisy and Gatsby danced. I remember being surprised by his graceful, conservative fox-trot—I had never seen him dance before.

Then they sauntered over to my house and sat on the steps for half an hour, while at her request, I remained watchfully in the garden.

Tom appeared from his oblivion as we were sitting down to supper together.

"Who is this Gatsby anyhow?" demanded Tom suddenly. "Some big bootlegger? He certainly must have strained himself to get this menagerie together."

"Lots of people come who haven't been invited," Daisy said suddenly. "They simply force their way in and he's too polite to object."

"I'd like to know who he is and what he does," insisted Tom. "And I think I'll make a point of finding out."

Daisy began to sing with the music in a husky, rhythmic whisper, bringing out a meaning in each word that it had never had before and would never have again.

It was when curiosity about Gatsby was at its highest that the lights in his house failed to go on one Saturday night. Wondering if he were sick, I went over to find out. Gatsby had dismissed every servant in his house the week before and replaced them with others.

"I wanted somebody who wouldn't gossip," he explained. "'Daisy comes over quite often—in the afternoons."

The next day Gatsby called me at Daisy's request—would I come to lunch at her house tomorrow? Miss Baker would be there. Half an hour later Daisy herself telephoned and seemed relieved that I was coming. Something was up.

When Gatsby and I arrived in the salon at Daisy's house, she and Jordan lay upon an enormous couch, like silver idols weighing down their own white dresses against the singing breeze of the fans.

When Tom left the room to get us drinks, Daisy went over to Gatsby and pulled his face down, kissing him on the mouth.

"You know I love you," she murmured.

"You forget there's a lady present," said Jordan.

Then Daisy remembered the heat and sat down guiltily on the couch just as a freshly laundered nurse leading a little girl came into the room.

"Bles-sed pre-cious," she crooned, holding out her arms. "Come to your own mother that loves you!"

The child, relinquished by the nurse, rushed across the room and rooted shyly into her mother's dress. Gatsby looked at the child with surprise. I don't think he had ever really believed in its existence before. Daisy sat back upon the couch. The nurse took a step forward and held out her hand. With a reluctant backward glance the well-disciplined child was pulled out the door.

We had luncheon in the dining-room, darkened too against the heat, and drank down nervous gayety with cold ale.

"What'll we do with ourselves this afternoon," cried Daisy, "and the day after that, and the next thirty years? . . . Let's all go to town!"

Gatsby's eyes floated toward her. "Ah," she cried, "you look so cool. You resemble the advertisement of the man," she went on innocently. "You know the advertisement of the man—"

Tom Buchanan saw. He was astounded. He looked at Gatsby, and then back at Daisy, as if he had just recognized her as someone he knew a long time ago.

"All right," broke in Tom quickly, "we're all going to town."

Tom came out of the house wrapping a quart bottle in a towel, followed by Daisy and Jordan wearing small tight hats of metallic cloth and carrying light capes over their arms.

"Shall we all go in my car?" suggested Gatsby.

"Well, you take my coupé and let me drive your car to town. Come on, Daisy, I'll take you in this circus wagon."

He opened the door but she moved outside the circle of his arm. . . . "You take Nick and Jordan. We'll follow you in the coupé," she said, as she moved towards Gatsby.

"Did you see that?" demanded Tom. "You think I'm pretty dumb, don't you?"

We were all irritable now with the fading ale, and aware of it, we drove for a while in silence. Then Doctor T. J. Eckleburg's faded eyes came into sight, Tom threw on both brakes impatiently and we slid to an abrupt dusty stop under Wilson's sign.

After a moment the proprietor emerged and gazed hollow-eyed at the car.
"What do you think we stopped for—to admire the view?" Tom asked impatiently.

"I'm sick," said Wilson. "Been sick all day. I need money pretty bad," he told Tom.
"I've been here too long. My wife and I want to go West."

"Your wife does!" exclaimed Tom, startled.

"She's been talking about it for ten years, and now she's going whether she wants to or not. I'm taking her away. I just got wised up to something funny the last two days. That's why I want to get away."

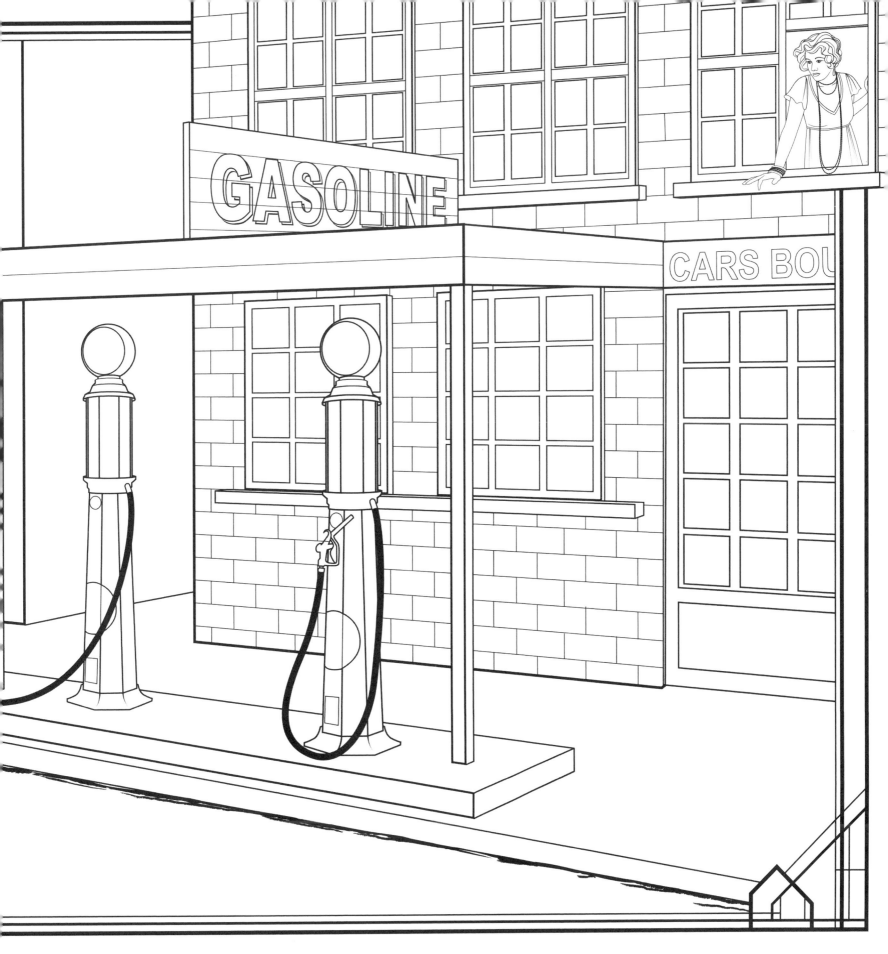

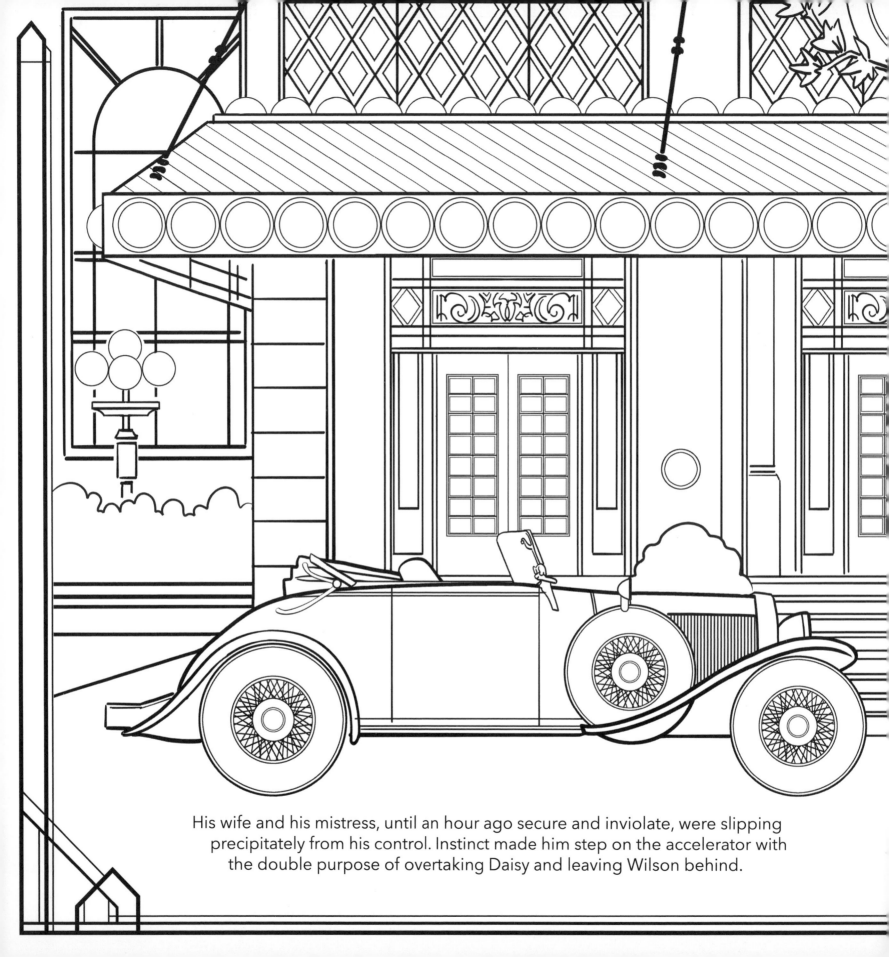

His wife and his mistress, until an hour ago secure and inviolate, were slipping precipitately from his control. Instinct made him step on the accelerator with the double purpose of overtaking Daisy and leaving Wilson behind.

At fifty miles an hour we came in sight of the easy-going blue coupé. As they drew up alongside, Tom said impatiently, "You follow me to the south side of Central Park, in front of the Plaza."

The prolonged and tumultuous argument about what to do to get out of the heat ended with our engaging the parlor of a suite in the Plaza Hotel, a place to have mint juleps. The room was large and stifling.

Tom started baiting Gatsby, asking questions about his earlier life. Daisy defended him, and the atmosphere became fraught with tension.

"I've got something to tell you, old sport," began Gatsby. "She's never loved you. She loves me."

Gatsby urged Daisy to confirm she had never loved Tom.

"Oh, you want too much!" she cried. "I love you now—isn't that enough? I loved him once, but I loved you, too."

 I glanced at Daisy, who was staring terrified between Gatsby and her husband. "Please, Tom. I can't stand this any more." Her frightened eyes told that whatever intentions, whatever courage she had had, were definitely gone.

"You two start on home, Daisy," said Tom. "In Mr. Gatsby's car."

The young Greek, Michaelis, who ran the coffee joint beside the ashheaps, was the principal witness at the inquest.

"I've got my wife locked in up there," explained Wilson calmly. "She's going to stay there till the day after tomorrow and then we're going to move away." Just as he was getting uneasy, some workmen came past the door bound for his restaurant, and Michaelis took the opportunity to get away.

When Michaelis came outside again, a little after seven, he heard Mrs. Wilson's voice, loud and scolding, downstairs in the garage. "Throw me down and beat me, you dirty little coward," she cried.

A moment later she rushed out into the dusk, waving her hands and shouting.

The "death car" as the newspapers called it, didn't stop; it came out of the gathering darkness, wavered tragically for a moment, and then disappeared around the next bend.

We saw the three or four automobiles and the crowd when we were still some distance away.

"Wreck!" said Tom. "That's good. Wilson'll have a little business at last."

He slowed down, but still without any intention of stopping, until, as we came nearer, the hushed, intent faces of the people at the garage door made him automatically put on the brakes.

"There's some bad trouble here," said Tom excitedly.

He reached up on tiptoes and peered over a circle of heads into the garage, to where he saw Myrtle Wilson's body, wrapped in a blanket, laying on a work-table.

"Auto hit her. Ins'antly killed," a policeman said. "She ran out ina road . . . didn't even stopus car."

We pushed through the still gathering crowd. Tom drove slowly until we were beyond the bend— then his foot came down hard. "The coward!" he whimpered. "He didn't even stop!"

The Buchanans' house floated suddenly toward us through the dark rustling trees.
Tom stopped beside the porch and looked up at the second floor, where two
windows bloomed with light among the vines.

"Daisy's home," he said. "I ought to have dropped you in West Egg,
Nick. There's nothing we can do tonight. I'll telephone for a
taxi to take you home."

I hadn't gone twenty yards when I heard my name and Gatsby stepped from between two bushes into the path.

"What are you doing?" I inquired.

"Just standing here, old sport. Did you see any trouble on the road?"

"Yes. . . . She was killed."

"I tried to swing the wheel—" He broke off, and suddenly, I guessed the truth. Daisy was driving.

"This woman rushed out. It seemed to me that she wanted to speak to us, thought we were somebody she knew. . . . Daisy stepped on it. I tried to make her stop. . . . She'll be okay tomorrow," he said.

"I got to West Egg by a side road" he went on, "and left the car in my garage. I don't think anybody saw us . . . I'm just going to wait and see if he tries to bother her . . . "

"I'll see if there's any sign of a commotion." I traversed the gravel softly, and tiptoed up the veranda steps. I came to the pantry window. Daisy and Tom were sitting opposite each other at the kitchen table, with plate of cold fried chicken between them, and two bottles of ale. Tom's hand had fallen upon and covered hers. There was an unmistakable air of natural intimacy about the picture, and anybody would have said that they were conspiring together.

As I tiptoed from the porch, I heard my taxi feeling its way along the dark road toward the house. Gatsby was waiting where I had left him in the drive.

"It's all quiet," I said. "Come home and get some sleep."

"I want to wait here till Daisy goes to bed. Good night, old sport."

So I walked away and left him standing there in the moonlight—
watching over nothing.

I couldn't sleep all night. I tossed half-sick between grotesque reality and savage, frightening dreams. Toward dawn I heard a taxi go up Gatsby's drive, and I jumped out of bed and dressed. Crossing his lawn, I saw the front door was still open, and he leaned against a table in the hall.

"Nothing happened," he said wanly. "I waited, and about 4:00 she came to the window and turned out the light."

"You ought to go away," I said. "It's pretty certain they'll trace your car."

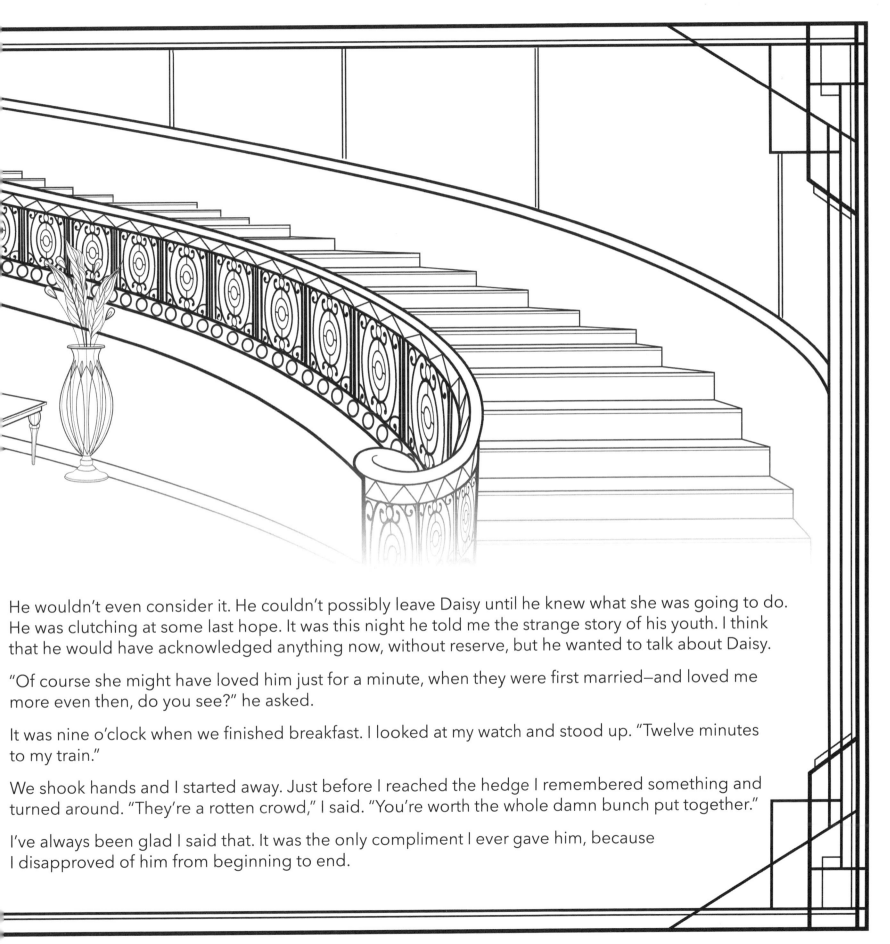

He wouldn't even consider it. He couldn't possibly leave Daisy until he knew what she was going to do. He was clutching at some last hope. It was this night he told me the strange story of his youth. I think that he would have acknowledged anything now, without reserve, but he wanted to talk about Daisy.

"Of course she might have loved him just for a minute, when they were first married—and loved me more even then, do you see?" he asked.

It was nine o'clock when we finished breakfast. I looked at my watch and stood up. "Twelve minutes to my train."

We shook hands and I started away. Just before I reached the hedge I remembered something and turned around. "They're a rotten crowd," I said. "You're worth the whole damn bunch put together."

I've always been glad I said that. It was the only compliment I ever gave him, because I disapproved of him from beginning to end.

Wilson's movements—he was on foot—were afterward traced. By half past two he was in West Egg, where he asked someone the way to Gatsby's house. So by that time he knew Gatsby's name.

At two o'clock Gatsby put on a bathing suit and informed the butler, if anyone phoned, word was to be brought to him at the pool.

No telephone message arrived, but the butler waited for it until four o'clock—until long after there was any one to give a message to if it came. The chauffeur heard the shots—afterward he could only say that he hadn't thought anything much about them.

After two years I remember the rest of that day, and that night and the next day, only as an endless drill of police and photographers and newspaper men in and out of Gatsby's front door. Someone with a positive manner, perhaps a detective, used the expression "madman" as he bent over Wilson's body that afternoon, and the adventitious authority of his voice set the key for the newspaper reports next morning.

I called up Dailsy half an hour after we found him. But she and Tom had gone away early that afternoon, and taken baggage with them.

"Left no address?" I asked, but there was none.

I wanted to get somebody for him. I called his friends and colleagues that I knew, but there were no responses.

I think it was the third day that the telegram signed Henry C. Gatz arrived from a town in Minnesota. It said only that the sender was leaving immediately and to postpone the funeral until he came.

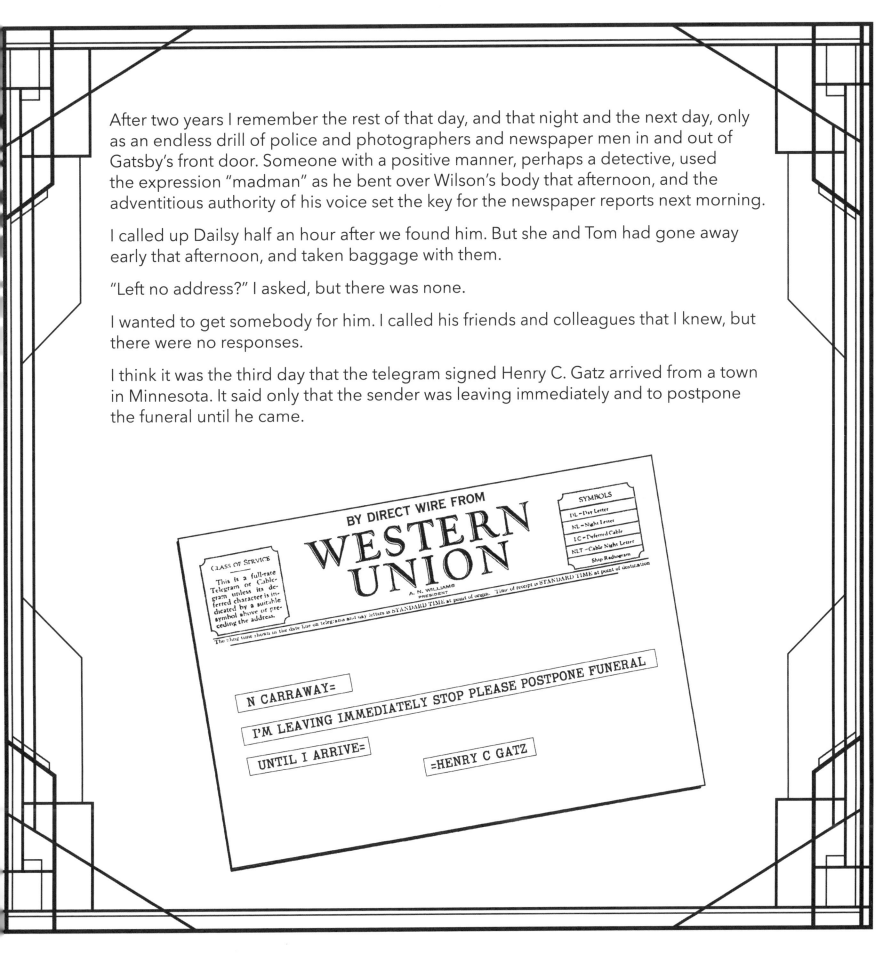

CLASS OF SERVICE

This is a full-rate Telegram or Cablegram unless its deferred character is indicated by a suitable symbol above or preceding the address.

BY DIRECT WIRE FROM

WESTERN UNION

A. N. WILLIAMS
PRESIDENT

The filing time shown in the date line on telegrams and day letters is STANDARD TIME at point of origin. Time of receipt is STANDARD TIME at point of destination

SYMBOLS

DL = Day Letter
NL = Night Letter
LC = Deferred Cable
NLT = Cable Night Letter
Ship Radiogram

N CARRAWAY=

I'M LEAVING IMMEDIATELY STOP PLEASE POSTPONE FUNERAL

UNTIL I ARRIVE=   =HENRY C GATZ

It was Gatsby's father. "I saw it in the Chicago newspaper," he said. He had reached an age where death no longer has the quality of ghastly surprise, and when he looked around him now for the first time and saw the height and splendor of the hall and great rooms, his grief began to be mixed with an awed pride.

"Jimmy sent me this picture." He took out his wallet with trembling fingers. It was a photograph of the house, cracked in the corners and dirty from many hands. "He come out to see me two years ago and bought me the house I live in now. Of course we was broke up when he run off from home, but I see now there was a reason for it. He knew he had a big future in front of him. And ever since he made a success he was very generous with me.

From his pocket he pulled out a ragged old copy of a book called Hopalong Cassidy. "Look here, this is a book he had when he was a boy. It just shows you".

He opened it at the back cover and turned it around for me to see. On the last fly-leaf was printed the word SCHEDULE, and the date September 12, 1906. And underneath was a detailed daily schedule.

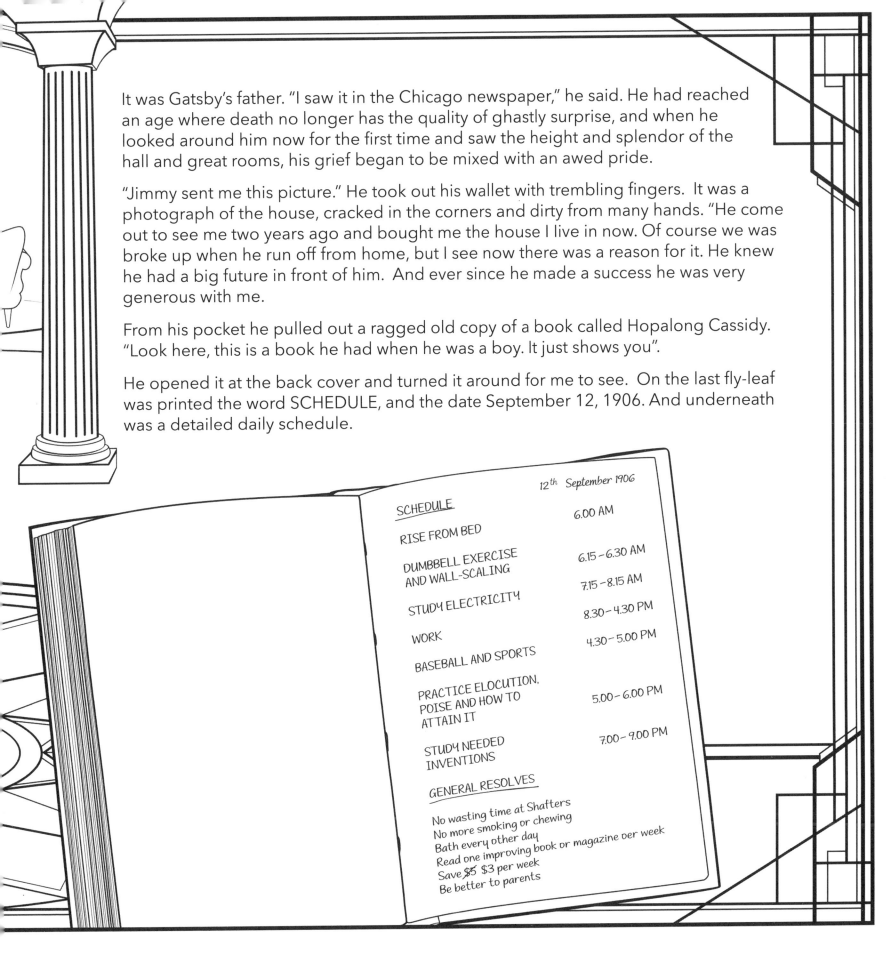

12th   September 1906

SCHEDULE

RISE FROM BED — 6.00 AM

DUMBBELL EXERCISE AND WALL-SCALING — 6.15 – 6.30 AM

STUDY ELECTRICITY — 7.15 – 8.15 AM

WORK — 8.30 – 4.30 PM

BASEBALL AND SPORTS — 4.30 – 5.00 PM

PRACTICE ELOCUTION, POISE AND HOW TO ATTAIN IT — 5.00 – 6.00 PM

STUDY NEEDED INVENTIONS — 7.00 – 9.00 PM

GENERAL RESOLVES

No wasting time at Shafters
No more smoking or chewing
Bath every other day
Read one improving book or magazine per week
Save $5 $3 per week
Be better to parents

The minister glanced several times at his watch, so I took him aside and asked him to wait for half an hour. But it wasn't any use. Nobody came.

About five o'clock our procession of three cars reached the cemetery—first a motor-hearse, then Mr. Gatz and the minister and I in the limousine, and a little later four or five servants and the postman from West Egg, in Gatsby's station wagon. Daisy hadn't sent a message or a flower.

One afternoon late in October I saw Tom Buchanan. He was walking ahead of me along Fifth Ave. Suddenly he saw me and walked back, holding out his hand.

"Tom," I inquired, "what did you say to Wilson that afternoon?"

He stared at me without a word, and I knew I had guessed right.

"I told him the truth," he said. "He came to the door while we were getting ready to leave. He tried to force his way upstairs. He was crazy enough to kill me if I hadn't told him who owned the car. His hand was on a revolver in his pocket every minute he was in the house. . . . And what if I did tell him? He ran over Myrtle like you'd run over a dog and never even stopped his car."

There was nothing I could say, except the one unutterable fact that it wasn't true.

"And if you think I didn't have my share of suffering—it was awful," he said.

I couldn't forgive him or like him, but I saw what he had done was, to him, entirely justified.

They were careless people, Tom and Daisy—they smashed up things and creatures and then retreated back into their money or their vast carelessness, or whatever it was that kept them together, and let other people clean up the mess they had made. . . .

Thunder Bay Press
An imprint of Printers Row Publishing Group
9717 Pacific Heights Blvd, San Diego, CA 92121
www.thunderbaybooks.com • mail@thunderbaybooks.com

Printers Row Publishing Group is a division of Readerlink Distribution Services, LLC.
Thunder Bay Press is a registered trademark of Readerlink Distribution Services, LLC.

Correspondence regarding the content of this book should be sent to Thunder Bay Press, Editorial Department, at the above address. Illustration inquiries should be sent to The Book Shop, Ltd., 7 Peter Cooper Rd, New York, New York 10010. www.thebookshopltd.com

Developed by The Book Shop Ltd.
Illustrations and cover design by Chellie Carroll
Designed by Eleanor Kwei

Thunder Bay Press
Publisher: Peter Norton • Associate Publisher: Ana Parker
Art Director: Charles McStravick
Senior Developmental Editor: April Graham Farr
Editor: Angela Garcia
Production Team: Mimi Oey, Rusty von Dyl

ISBN: 978-1-64517-479-0

Printed in China

25 24 23 22 21   1 2 3 4 5

Based on the novel The Great Gatsby *by F. Scott Fitzgerald; text has been abridged by The Book Shop, Ltd.*